PICNIC WITH PIGGINS

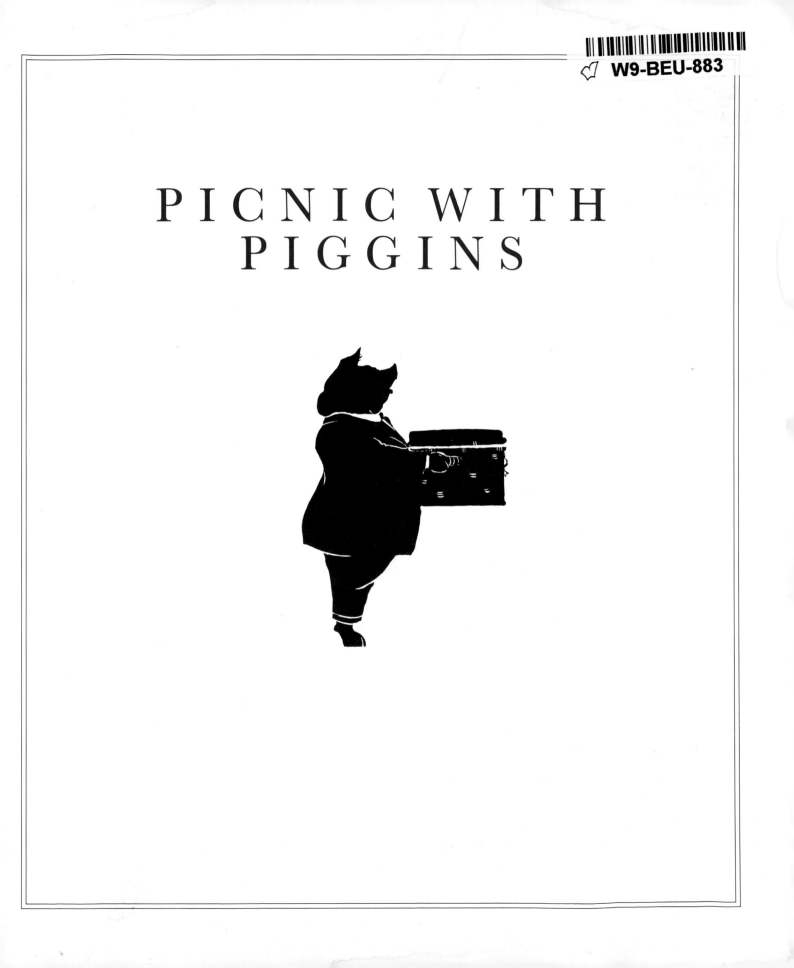

W9-BEU-883

PICNIC WITH PIGGINS

BY JANE YOLEN

ILLUSTRATED BY JANE DYER

HARCOURT BRACE & COMPANY

San Diego   New York   London

For David and Tom
just because

Text copyright © 1988 by Jane Yolen
Illustration copyright © 1988 by Jane Dyer

All rights reserved. No part of this publication
may be reproduced or transmitted in any form or
by any means, electronic or mechanical, including
photocopy, recording, or any information storage
and retrieval system without permission in
writing from the publisher.

Requests for permission to make copies of any
part of the work should be mailed to:
Permissions Department,
Harcourt Brace & Company, 6277 Sea Harbor Drive,
Orlando, Florida 32887-6777.

Voyager Books is a registered trademark of
Harcourt Brace & Company.

Library of Congress Cataloging-in-Publication Data
Yolen, Jane.
Picnic with Piggins.
Summary: A picnic in the country develops a mystery
which turns out to be a birthday surprise.
[1. Mystery and detective stories. 2. Pigs—
Fiction. 3. Birthdays—Fiction.]
I. Dyer, Jane, ill. II. Title.
PZ7.Y78Ph 1988   [E]   87-13564
ISBN 0-15-261534-2
ISBN 0-15-261535-0 (pbk.)

B D F G E C

The illustrations in this book were done in
colored pencil and Dr. Martin's watercolors on
140-lb. Fabriano hot-press watercolor paper.

The display type was set in Baskerville and
the text type was set Baskerville No. 2 by
Thompson Type, San Diego, California.

Color separations were made by Heinz Weber, Inc.
Printed and bound by
South China Printing Co., Ltd., Hong Kong

Production supervision by Warren Wallerstein
and Ginger Boyer
Designed by Camilla Filancia
based on a design by Dalia Hartman

Trit-trot, trit-trot. That is the sound of Piggins, the butler
at 47 The Meadows, going up the stairs.

UPSTAIRS   Mrs. Reynard helps Nanny Bess dress the children.

"Now that you are over the fox pox," says Mrs. Reynard to her two oldest kits, "you can play outside again. All too soon it will be time to go back to school. I have planned a special picnic. Piggins will go, too. Now listen carefully. . . ."

Rexy and Trixy clap their paws. They love doing things with Piggins. They know he is more than a butler. He was a hero in the Boar War. He has solved mysteries. And, with a bit of persuading, he can be made to sing.

BELOW STAIRS   Cook packs the picnic hamper. She puts in cheese and carrots, meats and pies, lettuce and celery sticks, and a great big Surprise. She will not mention the Surprise to Piggins.

Sara, the scullery maid, scrubs all the pots and pans. She looks as if she could use a scrubbing herself. Jane polishes the silver.

IN THE HALL   Piggins sets out the children's walking sticks and hats. Even though it is summer, he knows it is best to be prepared.

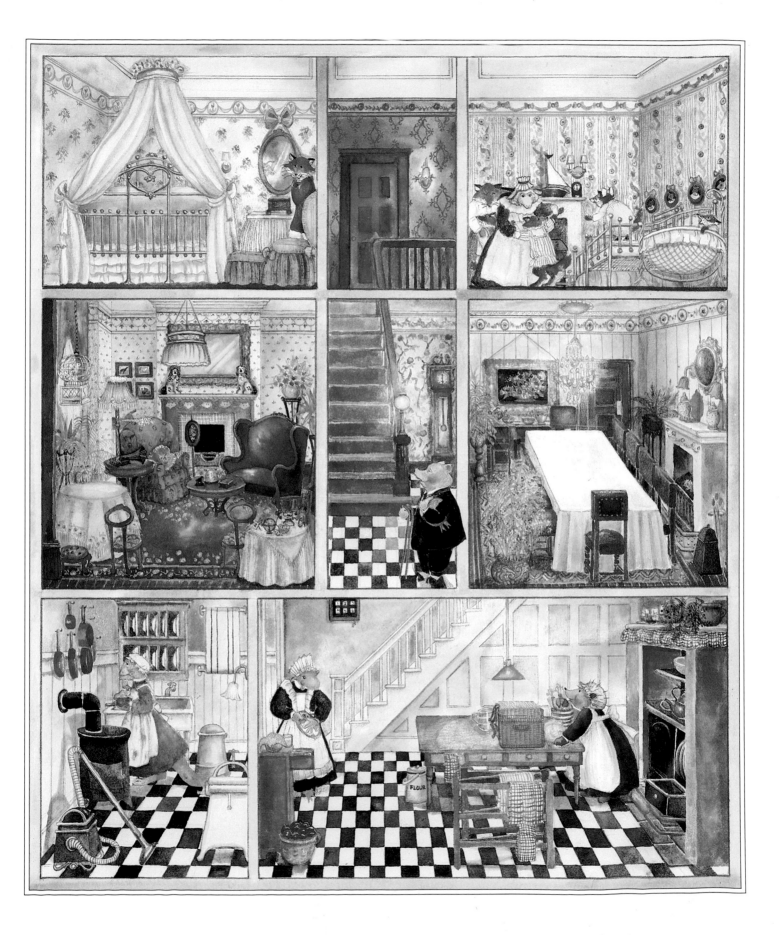

Aaaa-OOOO-ga. Aaaa-OOOO-ga. Down the street comes the
motorcar of the world-famous explorer Pierre Lapin and his three
unmarried sisters. They will be driving Piggins and the Reynard
kits to the picnic. They know all about the plans for the day, and
they will be in charge.

"I just love picnics," says the eldest Miss Lapin.

"All those carrot sticks," says one of her younger sisters.

"All that lettuce," says the other.

Pierre tips his hat at a passing carriage. "Picnics with Piggins!" he shouts. "They are always full of interesting surprises."

Rexy and Trixy tumble down the stairs and into the motorcar. They wave good-bye to their mother. Rexy squeezes in between two of the Lapin sisters. Trixy sits up front with Pierre and blows the horn.

Aaaa-OOOO-ga. Aaaa-OOOO-ga.

Piggins climbs into the front seat with the picnic hamper. Then off they go down the country lane.

The day is warm and sunny. Speedwell and wild rose bloom by the roadside. The woods are full of birdsongs and the tallyhos of a local fox hunt.

There is a graceful willow by the meandering river where they always picnic.

As Piggins spreads a blanket and begins to unpack the hamper, the Misses Lapin dangle their feet in the water. Trixy throws rose petals into the river. The petals quickly float away.

Rexy listens to Pierre Lapin tell a story of adventure on the high seas. There are pirates in the story and a princess as pink as a rose petal. Pierre rescues the princess.

"Is the story true?" asks Rexy.

"All my stories are true," says Pierre Lapin.

"Except for the ones that are not," calls out his eldest sister.

They all laugh. Even Pierre.

After playing a vigorous game of shuttlecock, they eat
everything in Cook's hamper. (Everything, that is, except the
Surprise, for there is a note saying they must save it until *just*
before they go home.) Then they settle in for a quiet spot of fishing.
But the game and the food have made everybody sleepy.

"Do not worry about Trixy and Rexy, Piggins," says Pierre Lapin. "I will take the first watch. I stayed up many sleepless nights when I was on the high seas."

Piggins nods gratefully and closes his eyes.

CRASH! SPLASH!

They all wake up with a start.

Trixy spots Rexy's hat in the middle of the river.

Pierre Lapin discovers that Rexy's fishing pole is in two pieces.

The Misses Lapin run up and down the river, looking for some sign of young Master Reynard. But except for a few popping bubbles way downstream, and the nearby tally-ho's of the fox hunt, there is no sound. No cries for help. No frantic gurgles. Even the birds have stopped singing.

"Oh, my!" cries the eldest Miss Lapin.

"Oh, my! oh, my!" cry her younger sisters.

"Oh, me! oh, my!" cries Pierre Lapin. His ears twist together and he wrings his paws.

Trixy says, "If Rexy's gone missing, can I have his piece of Cook's Surprise?"

Piggins says nothing, but his face is very stern, and he looks around and listens with great care.

"Do you think Rexy has been kit-napped?" asks the eldest Miss Lapin.

"He must have been," says Trixy. "That is his favorite hat. Rexy would never let anything happen to it." She points dramatically to the hat in the river.

"Clue number one!" says Pierre Lapin.
Piggins says nothing.

"Do you think he may be hurt?" asks one of the younger Misses
Lapin.

Trixy holds up the two pieces of the fishing pole. "He must have put up an awful struggle," she says. "Poor Rexy!"

"Clue number two!" says Pierre Lapin.

Piggins says nothing.

"Look! I have found his walking stick," cries the other Miss Lapin. "Up here by the riverbank."

"Do not touch it," Pierre warns. "There may be pawprints. Or perhaps Rexy has left it behind to point the way."

"Brave, brave Rexy," says the eldest Miss Lapin.

"I definitely think brave Rexy would want me to have his slice of Surprise," says Trixy. "Don't you?"

"Clue number three!" says Pierre Lapin.

Piggins says nothing.

"Is there a ransom note?" asks Pierre Lapin.

"Of course! A ransom note!" cry the three Misses Lapin as they hold on to one another and weep loudly. "There is always a ransom note."

"I will look in the picnic hamper," says Trixy. "Next to Cook's Surprise. Perhaps there is a ransom note there."

She looks and indeed there *is* a note.

Pierre reads it aloud:

IF YOU WANT TO SEE REXY AGAIN,

PIGGINS MUST WALK DOWN THE ROAD ALONE,

AND HE MUST SING A SONG SO WE KNOW

HE IS ON HIS WAY.

"How odd," says the eldest Miss Lapin. "The kit-nappers must know that Piggins can be trusted."

"And they must know that he can sing," adds Trixy. She smiles at Pierre Lapin.

"Odd indeed," says Piggins.

"Quite a puzzle," agrees Pierre Lapin.

"Not a puzzle at all," says Piggins, "but a hoax."

"A hoax?" the others all cry. "Why, merciful heavens! Whatever do you mean?"

"What about the clues?" asks Pierre Lapin.

Piggins smiles. "Clue number one. Notice that Rexy's favorite hat has not moved one inch down the river. It is not caught on anything we can see. But *something* is holding it."

"Oh," says Pierre Lapin. His cheeks are pink.

"Clue number two," says Piggins. "The broken rod is not broken at all, but only neatly unhinged."

"Unhinged!" cry the three Lapin sisters. They twist their kerchiefs and look nearly unhinged themselves.

"Clue number three," says Piggins. "The walking stick. Since I am not supposed to touch it, I want to touch it very much indeed." He picks up the stick, and there is a piece of fishing line attached to it. When he pulls on the string, he reels in Rexy's hat.

"What about the ransom note?" asks Trixy.

Piggins smiles again. "I believe I know the song you want me to sing, my dear hoaxers." He turns and walks down the road, singing at the top of his lungs:

HAPPY BIRTHDAY TO YOU,
HAPPY BIRTHDAY TO YOU,
HAPPY BIRTHDAY DEAR . . .

"Piggins!" everyone joins in.

Suddenly the woods are filled with the members of the local hunt. "Surprise!" they shout as they leap up and scream.

Rexy jumps from his horse, yelling the loudest of all.

Trixy carries Cook's birthday cake Surprise to Piggins, who cuts it and gives everyone a slice.

"We thought a birthday mystery would be the best present of all," says Mrs. Reynard. "Only we never expected you to solve it so quickly. You *almost* spoiled the surprise. Naughty Piggins!"

After they eat the cake, they all head for home.

UPSTAIRS   Trixy and Rexy get ready for bed. Trixy takes a handkerchief out of her pocket. In it is an extra piece of the birthday cake. She shares it with her little sisters, who still have the fox pox.

IN THE LIVING ROOM   Mr. and Mrs. Reynard sit by the fire, drinking tea.

"Such a lovely day," says Mrs. Reynard. "But next year we must try harder to surprise him." She laughs. "Perhaps you could invent a surprise machine."

"Perhaps I shall, my dear," says Mr. Reynard.

BELOW STAIRS   Sarah has cleaned up the picnic basket. She could do with a good cleaning herself. Cook snoozes in her chair. Jane has put the kettle on the stove for one last cup of tea.

IN THE HALL   Piggins locks the front door of 47 The Meadows. He hears the kettle whistling.

It has been quite the happiest birthday Piggins can remember. He is tired but smiling. With Rexy's hat in hand, he goes down the stairs. He will have to get it clean for the next day. *Trit-trot, trit-trot, trit-trot.*